Song Writer's Manuscript Book

6 Stave
Extra Space Between Each Stave for Lyric Writing
32 Pages

WWW.MELBAY.COM

MEL BAY PUBLICATIONS, INC.

MEL BAY PUBLICATIONS, INC.

MEL BAY PUBLICATIONS, INC.

MEL BAY PUBLICATIONS, INC.

MEL BAY PUBLICATIONS, INC.

MEL BAY PUBLICATIONS, INC.

MEL BAY PUBLICATIONS, INC.

MEL BAY PUBLICATIONS, INC.

MEL BAY PUBLICATIONS, INC.